PARADISE HOUSE

Keeping COTTON Tail

PARADISE HOUSE
Keeping
COTTON
TaiL

HILARY McKAY

Illustrated by Tony Kenyon

Hodder
Children's
Books

a division of Hodder Headline

Chapter One

Anna and Nathan and Danny and Old McDonald, the caretaker, were clearing out the empty flat at Paradise House. New people were coming to live in it.

"New people! New people! New people!" sang Anna. The empty flat was across the landing from where she lived with her mother and father and it was exciting to think of it being used at last.

"They might be awful," said Nathan.

"Yes," said Anna.

"Well then!"

"They'll still be new," said Anna cheerfully.

Danny did not see what all the fuss was about. All this cleaning and clearing and wondering and talking, and in the end, whoever they were, they would just be people. Danny preferred animals. He stretched out on an ancient orange sofa and pretended to go to sleep.

"Now, you can just wake up again, Young Danny!" said Old McDonald, looking down at him. "I thought you was here to help! There's all this lot to shift before tomorrow and where it's to go I don't know!"

That was the trouble. The empty flat was full of junk and it all belonged to Old McDonald. It was things that he did not want himself, but could not quite bear to throw away. Now that the new people were coming the junk had to go, but Old McDonald still could not quite make himself throw it away. He thumped noisily round the empty flat, shoving things from one place to another and then shoving them back again, and all the time grumbling crossly to himself. Old McDonald was a very stubborn old man, and quite alarmingly bad tempered. Danny could

remember a time when he had been scared of him but that was long, long ago. The Paradise House children had made friends with Old McDonald in spite of his temper.

We tamed him, remembered Danny, still sprawled comfily on the sofa with his feet up higher than his head. It had been rather like taming a rhinoceros, he thought, and he said out loud, "If I ever have one I shall call it Old McDonald!"

"One what?" asked Anna.

"A rhinoceros."

"I'll give you rhinoceros!" said Old McDonald, jerking open a pair of curtains and shaking out clouds of dust. "Rhinoceros indeed! Lovely, I *don't* think!"

"Well, a camel then," said Danny. "But it would have to be the right sort. The ones with short legs and only one hump . . ."

Old McDonald gave a very camel-like snort.

"I should love a camel! I wish Paradise House wasn't *No Pets Allowed*!"

"Rules are rules," said Old McDonald, "and a good thing too! We don't want no camels called Old McDonald around here, thank you very much!"

"That *No Pets Allowed* rule isn't fair, I don't think," remarked Nathan, who was going through a box of old saucepans to see which one fitted best on his head. "It should be the same for everyone and it's not. You've got a cat."

"It's not my cat," said Old McDonald, dumping the curtains onto a box of old books and straightening up to look round the room. "It's a cat that drops by to visit! Anyway, I don't have to go by the same rules as you lot do! I'm a caretaker, which is a responsible position, whereas you are tenants, what might get out of hand! Now then, Danny, you've given me an idea! Get up off that sofa and take a corner with Nathan."

"What are you going to do with it?"

"We'll take it to your mum, seeing as you seem to like it so much! Waste not, want not!

It's much too good to throw out! We'll bump it up one stair at a time and see what she says. You bring that beady curtain if you're coming with us, Anna! She can have that as well!"

Old McDonald was good at getting his own way. Very soon the sofa was parked outside the flat that Danny shared with his mother.

"But I don't *want* a sofa!" she exclaimed, backing away in horror when she saw it. "I haven't *room* for a sofa!"

"Take up no space at all!" said Old McDonald.

"Of course it will! I'm sorry but you will have to take it away! Please stop shaking those horrible beads at me, Anna!"

"That's another thing we brought for you," said Old McDonald firmly. "A nice bright fly curtain! You don't want flies all over the place!"

"I haven't *got* . . ."

"And the sofa will go very snug under your window if you get rid of the rubbish you got

piled up there! Them nasty ferns that bring
in the damp! Anyway, it's here now and I
must get on!"

"But I *won't* have it!" wailed Danny's mother. "I *won't*! Look at it! Filthy! Stop laughing, Danny! And the colour! Orange! And full of dust! Poof!" She disappeared into a grey cloud as she slapped it, and then began sneezing and sneezing.

"A bit of a brush and it'll be good as new," said Old McDonald heartlessly as he headed back down the stairs. "And it's not cost you a penny! A present . . ."

"A present!" screeched Danny's mother. "A *present*! Come *back*!"

"Time was, people said, 'Thank you!' " remarked Old McDonald, taking no notice at all. "Now then, Anna! Your dad's a great reader! I've a big box of books that'll just do for him. Let's get them across!"

Anna's father was out but her mother was in and she was no more pleased with her present than Danny's mother had been.

"They're *dreadful*!" she said. "They *smell*! They're *mouldy*! I don't expect anyone's read them for years and years and years!"

"What's a bit of mould?" asked Old McDonald, while Anna and Nathan and Danny nearly fell over laughing. "Those books was my Uncle Bob's and he had them from his grandad and that must make them just about antique! I've brought across a parcel of old curtains that'll do you very nice as well! Proper heavy ones, not like the flimsy bits you got hanging up now! Shall I put this lot into the sitting room for you then?"

"*No!*" said Anna's mother, so Old McDonald pushed it all into the kitchen instead and hurried quickly away to take two rolls of dingy carpet and six battered saucepans to Nathan's home downstairs.

"Oh," said Nathan's mother, very uncheerfully. "But I think I have enough saucepans!"

"No proper decent cook ever has enough saucepans," said Old McDonald reprovingly. "And I've got something here very special for young Chloe!"

Chloe was Nathan's baby sister. She was

one year old. She and Old McDonald were very alike and they got on well together. Chloe's present was a large wood-wormy rocking horse.

"Mine, mine, mine!" shrieked Chloe in delight the moment she saw it. "Mine, mine, mine, mine, mine!"

"Mine" was the only word that Chloe had learned so far. She used it all the time, but especially in shops.

"Mine!" said Chloe triumphantly when Old McDonald lifted her onto the saddle.

"That's what I call a proper thank you!" said Old McDonald.

The rest of the junk in the empty flat was loaded into black bin bags. Old McDonald took them down to the Miss Kent sisters. They were two old ladies who lived on the ground floor opposite Nathan's family.

"You will remember when this was the latest fashion!" said Old McDonald as he handed over the bin bags, and the Miss Kents, dreadfully offended, said, "Indeed They Did Not!"

"Let us hope," said Old McDonald, as he locked the empty, junk-free flat at the end of the day, "that this new family has manners and knows when to be grateful! We'll find out the worst tomorrow, I suppose."

Chapter Two

"Horrible!" said Anna.

"Horrible *and* rude!" said Nathan.

"Horrible *and* rude *and* fierce!" said Danny.

"She's called Kathy. Kathy Cotton. She's starting at our school when we go back next week. Her mum told my mum."

"Will she be in our class?"

"Probably."

Danny and Nathan groaned.

The new family had arrived. Dozens of boxes. A jumble of furniture. Scarlet geraniums. The smell of coffee where no coffee had ever been before. A clatter of strange voices. A father and a mother

and a red-headed girl.

The red-headed girl had hair that stood up in spikes. She wore an enormous old black jacket. She stamped into the entrance hall of Paradise House with her head down and her hands stuck deep into her jacket pockets and said, "This dump stinks!"

She caught sight of Anna and Nathan and Danny watching from the stairs and demanded stormily, "What d'you think you're staring at?"

They were still trying to think of a squashing enough reply when she barged across the hall, stumbled over Chloe (who was under everyone's feet as usual) and knocked her down flat.

"You be careful of my sister!" said Nathan angrily, running down the stairs to pick Chloe up.

"*You* be careful of your sister!" said the girl, who stuck out her tongue, marched upstairs, kicked open the empty flat door, and kicked it shut again behind her.

"Sorry," said the girl's father, smiling apologetically at Nathan and Chloe over a pile of boxes that he was carrying. "Take no notice of Kathy! She's a bit upset. Is the little girl all right?"

"I'll take her to Mum," said Nathan, but Chloe would not let herself be taken. She copied exactly what Kathy had done, folded her arms across her chest, stuck out her tongue, marched across the hall, kicked at her door until Nathan opened it, and stamped inside.

The door closed very jerkily, as Chloe, with a lot of puffing, slowly kicked it shut.

"Oh dear!" said Kathy's father.

Kathy did not appear again for ages and ages.

"She's scared!" said Danny. "Good!"

"I think she's ashamed," said Anna. "Anyway, she ought to be!"

"I bet she isn't," said Nathan. "I bet she's not scared either. Her parents are probably just not letting her out! Keeping her prisoner! I don't blame them!"

This turned out to be partly true. Over cups of tea at Anna's flat Kathy's parents revealed that she had locked herself in her bedroom.

"Sulking?" asked Anna.

"Almost definitely sulking," said Kathy's mother, her eyes twinkling at Anna. "She has done nothing else for weeks."

Later, drinking coffee and eating biscuits brought down by Danny's mum, they all nodded quite cheerfully at a tightly closed door and said that it seemed the worst was over.

"But listen to her in there!" said Danny. "Bashing and thumping and talking to herself!"

"Nothing to the scenes we had yesterday!" said Kathy's father.

At suppertime (pizza and salad) with Nathan's family, they said "Not to worry. All in good time," and they left Kathy sandwiches and the biscuit tin in case she got hungry.

"So long as she's eating," remarked

Nathan's father rather heartlessly, stroking the bump on Chloe's head.

"She'll be fine when she's made some friends," said Kathy's mother.

"Hasn't she got any then?" asked Nathan, who was then asked if he would like to leave the table.

"Yes please!" he said at once, and escaped before they could change their minds. Nathan went and called for Anna and Danny, and they had a meeting together on the front doorstep to compare notes.

"Sulking for weeks!"

"Crashing and thumping and talking to herself!"

"Stuffing biscuits in her bedroom!"

"Poor old Chloe!"

"I said the new people might be awful! I told you so, Anna!"

"Her mum and dad are all right," said Anna fairly.

"Good job too! She's bad enough for all three!"

"Ho!" said Old McDonald, suddenly appearing on the basement steps and making everybody jump. "I've been listening to you! All on to one! Very nice, I must say! Since when were you perfect?"

Anna, Danny and Nathan rushed to defend themselves.

"She started it!"

"She knocked over my sister! Now Chloe's got a great lump!"

"Three on to one is disgraceful," said Old McDonald virtuously, heading back down his basement steps. "And if I catch you at it I'll have your livers!"

"But . . ."

"Not another word!"

They waited, listening for the basement door to shut. It didn't.

"Ho!" said Old McDonald triumphantly out of the darkness.

Anna looked out of her bedroom window that night and she saw a strange thing. Kathy

Cotton, still wrapped up in her jacket, prowling round the dusky garden. Every now and then she would whip a hand out of a pocket and yank up a clump of grass. She was stuffing her pockets full of grass.

Anna stared and stared and then Kathy saw her. Her eyes went big and frightened and suddenly Anna was sorry for this strange new girl. She waved, just as she might have waved to Danny or Nathan, but Kathy did not wave back. Instead, very slowly, she pulled one

hand out of her pocket. She pointed a finger at Anna and then made her hand into a mouth, opening and shutting.

'*You tell!*' said Kathy's signs to Anna.

Kathy pointed to herself. '*I!*'

She pointed back to Anna and with one finger drew a slow long line across her throat.

Oh! thought Anna, very startled. Oh! And then she suddenly thought, Tell what? About Kathy being in a garden at night? About stuffing her pockets with grass? About how frightened she had seemed when she saw someone watching?

Tell what? wondered Anna, as she climbed into bed.

She could hardly wait to finish her breakfast before rushing over to Kathy's flat the next morning. She banged on the door and after a long, long time it was opened just a crack by Kathy herself. She still wore her awful black jacket and she was bent almost double, one arm hugging her stomach.

"Clear off!" she said to Anna.

"I came to tell you I wouldn't tell! Only *what* am I not to tell?"

"Mind your own business," said Kathy, bending lower than ever.

"Are you ill?" asked Anna, quite alarmed.

Kathy opened her mouth to answer, and then suddenly jerked to her knees.

"Go away!" she yelled desperately, but she was too late. Anna had seen. A black and white rabbit. A *large* black and white rabbit. A large black and white rabbit had dropped out from under Kathy's jacket and had been grabbed and stuffed back under all in the blinking of an eye.

Kathy gave a great gulping sob and Anna spun round and checked the staircase behind her. There was no one about and the room behind Kathy seemed empty too, except for the chaos of unpacking.

"No one saw!" she whispered. "Don't start crying! They'll only wonder why! Where are they?"

"Who?" asked Kathy, staring and sniffing and clutching the front of her jacket which was wriggling as if it was alive.

"Your parents, of course!"

"Mum's in the shower and Dad's gone out to buy paint."

"Didn't you know that Paradise House was no pets allowed?"

"Of course I did!" Kathy's jacket seemed to be settling down and she was beginning to sound cross again. "I've known for ages! I . . ."

"Kathy!"

A door suddenly opened and Kathy's mother appeared in a cloud of steam.

"I thought I heard someone! Anna, how nice of you to call! Come right in and have a drink! Kathy, I put some Coke in the fridge last night. Take that silly jacket off before you cook in it and go and fetch some Coke for Anna! And bring the biscuit tin too! And . . ."

"Please," interrupted Anna, seeing the

hunted expression on Kathy's face, "can Kathy come with me? Right now, I mean! She wants to, don't you, Kathy?"

Kathy sighed with relief and nodded.

"I could show her Paradise House. Or the garden. But it's quite cold in the garden. For August, I mean. Good job she's got her jacket on . . ."

Anna saw that Kathy's mother was staring at her as if she was mad and her voice trailed away. She paused, wondering what she could say next, and Kathy took over.

"Come on," she said suddenly, pushed past Anna, and headed as fast as she could down the stairs.

Kathy's mother turned to Anna, obviously bursting with questions, but Anna was already backing away.

"I'll just shut the door, shall I?" she asked, before Kathy's mother could begin to protest.

"Well, but . . ."

"Goodbye," said Anna, very firmly and politely, thinking it best to pretend she hadn't heard, and closed the door and ran.

In the entrance hall she caught up with Kathy and pushed her into the cupboard under the stairs. This was a place that Anna and Danny and Nathan used when they needed somewhere private to meet. Old McDonald kept his buckets and mops and old newspapers in there, and he had guarded it very fiercely until Chloe was born. Then, when Nathan had been almost driven out of his home by her screams, old McDonald had allowed him to take refuge among the mops. The children had used it ever since. It was quite a good den, if you didn't mind spiders and Old McDonald, who was always in and out.

Anna switched on the light, shoved Kathy down onto a pile of newspapers and said eagerly, "Show him to me again! I only saw him for a second when we were upstairs."

"D'you *promise* you won't tell?"

"Of course I won't! I didn't tell your mum, did I?"

"I s'pose not!" admitted Kathy.

"Go on then!"

"All right."

Kathy unzipped her jacket, which immediately made her look much smaller and thinner, and there was the rabbit, large-eyed and blinking, and as black and white and fluffy as a cuddly toy come to life.

"He's called Cotton Tail," said Kathy, her voice husky and secret. "That's a sort of joke, because of my name. Kathy Cotton, you see. My friend's rabbit had four babies and they called them Flopsy, Mopsy, Cotton Tail and Peter. They kept Flopsy and they sold Mopsy and Peter, and I had Cotton Tail for my birthday when I was seven."

"He's beautiful!"

"Yes. But when we had to move here my mum and dad said I'd got to give him back."

"To your friend who gave him to you?"

"Yes, to Spike. And I said I wouldn't and I

fought and fought and went on and on at them, but they made me. They said they couldn't help it!"

Kathy glanced at Anna to see what she was thinking, and Anna noticed how dark and furious her eyes had become.

"Could they help it?" she asked.

"They could have found somewhere to move to that wasn't no pets allowed. But they wouldn't. They liked this place. They said there was a good school and a garden and children just my age to make . . . to make . . ."

"Friends?" said Anna.

"So they took Cotton Tail down to Spike's, with his hutch and everything. Last week, so I could visit him every day and get used to not having him gradually. That's what they said. But I didn't get used to it. And the last day before we moved here I went to see him and Spike was out, and his parents were out and Cotton Tail was in his hutch in their back garden and I just took him. And I left the door open, like he'd run away."

"They'll think he's escaped and not dare to tell you."

"That's what I thought."

"Poor Spike!"

"I know. But as soon as I found somewhere safe to keep him I was going to write and tell him it was all right. I thought there might be somewhere here. A big old house they said it was. I thought there might be secret corners and I could buy another hutch. But there are people everywhere! *Everywhere!* And now I can't even stay in my bedroom with him. They're decorating it, to cheer me up. I don't know what to do!"

Just then there were voices outside. Danny and Nathan and Old McDonald.

"What's your mum done with that very nice sofa then?"

"She shoved it into my bedroom. There isn't room to move!"

"Not a word of thanks! A sofa in your

bedroom, and not a word of thanks! When I was a boy bedrooms had beds in, and that was all!"

"Lucky you!" said Danny.

"No gratitude! Young Chloe is the only one of you that knows what it means."

"She nearly broke my leg with that rocking horse this morning," said Nathan. "My mum says it's a menace!"

"Graceless *and* thankless!" said Old McDonald, stomping away.

Chapter Three

Kathy and Anna sat in the cupboard and held their breath and waited for the boys to go. This did not happen. Instead they heard a voice faraway: Nathan's mother.

"Nathan! Nathan! Just come here and keep an eye on your sister for a minute!"

"Quick!" the girls heard Nathan say to Danny. "Hide, or we'll end up looking after Chloe all morning!"

"Nathan!"

Nathan's mother called again. Kathy and Anna heard the sound of hurrying feet and then the cupboard door flew open. Nathan dived inside and a moment later Danny followed after him.

"Crikey!" exclaimed Nathan, catching sight of Cotton Tail and gazing in delight. "Crikey! Good grief! A rabbit! Whose rab . . ."

"It's my rabbit," interrupted Kathy from the back of the cupboard.

"Oh," said Nathan in a very different, very unfriendly voice. "*Your* rabbit. Oh. My sister's got a great big bump where you knocked her over yesterday."

"I didn't mean to!" Kathy said defensively. "She was right under my feet before I even saw her. And if I'd stopped I would have dropped my rabbit. He was under my jacket."

"You didn't even say sorry!"

"*You* didn't even say hello! You just stood there in a row, staring and staring!"

"Don't start quarrelling!" ordered Anna in a loud whisper.

"Yes, shut up," agreed Danny, squatting down as quietly as he could and holding out his hand for Cotton Tail to sniff. "You'll frighten him. He's a real beauty! Hello, Rabbit!"

Animals usually seemed to like Danny. Kathy's rabbit came over at once to be stroked and Kathy became much less fierce when she saw how gentle Danny was with him.

"He's called Cotton Tail," she said. "And I *didn't* mean to knock your baby over!"

"All right, you didn't," agreed Nathan. "Anyway, Chloe's all right, she's very tough! And she falls over all the time! I suppose Anna's told you that if Old McDonald sees that rabbit he'll go state-of-the-art bonkers?"

"Yes."

"How did it get here anyway?"

Kathy explained all over again how she had kidnapped Cotton Tail back from her friend Spike, and how she had travelled all the way from Kent with him stuffed up her jacket, hoping to find a place to keep him safe.

"Poor Spike!" said Danny, just as Anna had done. "But I know a place where he could stay and be safe! In my attic! At least, he could next week when Mum goes back to

work. She's off till the end of this holiday, but he could go up there after that."

"Couldn't he now?" asked Kathy, and was surprised at how emphatically Danny and Nathan and Anna shook their heads.

"Mum's paranoid about that attic," said Danny. "She starts getting twitchy every time she hears a sound! She's been like it for ages, ever since Anna and I had our zoo up there."

"Ever since Anna and you shifted all those tiles and the roof blew off, you mean!" said Nathan. "Anyway, what are you going to do until next week? What about keeping him in here?"

That question was answered almost at once. Outside in the hall a door flew open and there was the sound of small, determined feet. Chloe knew where to find her brother, even if their mother did not. A minute later her fingers appeared around the edge of the door, which could never be completely shut because it only opened from the outside.

"Quick, Kathy!" exclaimed Anna.

Kathy grabbed Cotton Tail to hide him out of sight, but Cotton Tail had had enough of the inside of jackets and did not want to be caught. By the time he was safely out of the way the cupboard door was wide open and Chloe had seen.

"Mine!" she shrieked, making a dive for Kathy and getting a grip on her hair. "Mine, mine . . ."

"Flipping kid!" muttered Nathan as he unprized her fingers one by one and dragged her off. "Ouch! Don't kick me!"

"Mine!" Chloe wailed, beating furiously at him with her hands and feet while her brother, clutching her round her stomach, backed slowly out of the cupboard. "MINE! MINE! MINE!"

Mrs Amadi, Nathan's mother, had come running at the first scream so she was on hand to take Chloe, still fighting, as Nathan emerged into the hall. She rolled her eyes up to the ceiling, nodded but did not try to speak, and carted Chloe away.

"I can't possibly keep Cotton Tail in here," said Kathy very firmly when Nathan was back inside. "And I can't keep him in our flat because Mum and Dad are decorating my bedroom and he can't go in Danny's attic until next week, you said. So where else is there?"

There was a long silence.

"Perhaps he could stay with me," suggested Anna eventually. "If it's only for a few days. In my bedroom, I mean."

"Your parents would notice straight away," objected Kathy.

"They wouldn't, Kathy!" Danny told her earnestly, while Nathan and Anna nodded in agreement. "You haven't seen Anna's bedroom! You could hide something much bigger than a rabbit in it!"

"It's such a mess," explained Nathan. "Toys and clothes and rubbish and papers and things in heaps everywhere! Her mum's given up, she told my mum . . ."

"Come and see!" said Anna, not at all upset

at this description, and led the way upstairs.

"You're not taking Kathy in *there*?" asked Anna's mother as Anna shepherded her friends through the little flat to her bedroom door. "Do you really think you should? She's not used to it like the rest of us. Whatever will she say?"

"She'll like it," said Anna cheerfully, pushing Kathy in in front of her.

"She'll think it's just right!" Danny agreed as he went after the girls.

"It *is* just right," said Nathan, following last and closing the door behind himself as he spoke. "There! He can't get out now, Kathy! Put him down and see what he does!"

Kathy did as she was told and soon saw that the room *was* just right. The bed was a heap of clutter, and the chair and table and chest of drawers were further heaps. The floor was ankle-deep, knee-deep in places, with clothes, toys, games, cardboard models, and dozens of cuddly toys. Cotton Tail blended in perfectly. He was hardly more noticeable than an extra teddy bear would have been.

"He's house trained," said Kathy, watching with more and more hope as Cotton Tail,

beautifully camouflaged, explored the room. "All you need is newspaper in a box he can jump in and out of and he uses that for a toilet. You just need to put down clean paper every day."

"What about food?" asked Danny.

"I've got a bag of rabbit food and he likes human food too. Carrots and apples and digestive biscuits. Things like that."

"It's going to be easy!" said Nathan.

At first it *was* easy. It really seemed that their plan might work. Anna and Kathy spent the day in Anna's bedroom, Danny and Nathan visited from time to time, and everyone said how nice it was that the children had made friends so soon. Then Anna's mother began sneezing. She sneezed and sneezed. By bedtime her nose was swollen and her eyes were streaming but the sneezing did not stop.

"Whatever can be the matter with me?" she groaned, sniffing and mopping and pressing her fingers tightly against the sides of her head.

Anna felt strangely guilty and could not think why. She knew quite well that she had not made her mother sneeze, but she could not get rid of the idea that it was somehow her fault. Then suddenly she caught sight of the box of dusty, mildewy books that she had helped Old McDonald unload the day before.

"I wonder if it could be these," she suggested, sniffing them cautiously.

Anna's mother had to sneeze eight or nine times before she could reply, but when she did she sounded more hopeful than she had all day.

"Why ever didn't I think of the books myself!" she exclaimed, and sent Anna hurrying down to the basement to explain to Old McDonald that he must come and take them all back.

"Try to tell him nicely!" she called after Anna as she ran down the stairs.

Anna tried, but discovered it was not

possible. Old McDonald was most offended and he came upstairs very slowly and grumpily. He was not at all pleased to have his books returned, and made many rude remarks about the bad manners of some people he could not mention.

"But they are making me ill!" protested Anna's mother.

"Never heard such rubbish in my life!" said Old McDonald, watching unmoved while Anna's mother blew her nose and wiped her eyes. "Any excuse!"

"They ought to be burnt!" Anna's mother fumbled open a new box of tissues and dragged out a handful. "Fusty and mildewy and full of dust!"

She stopped again to sneeze, and Old McDonald gazed impatiently up at the ceiling as if to say it was all put on.

"I really *don't* mean to upset you . . ."

"Ho!" said Old McDonald. "It would take more than that to upset me! Rudeness is commonplace these days!"

"Oh dear! Oh dear! Oh dear!" said Anna's mother, sneezing worse than ever when Old McDonald had gone. "I'm sorry, Anna, but I do feel so dreadful! I think I'd better go to bed!"

Anna went to bed too, and was only slightly disturbed by the sound of Cotton Tail hopping silently round the room from time to time. In the morning she startled her mother by appearing with an armload of laundry, collected from the floor before her mother could appear and start poking around the bedroom for herself.

Her mother was still sneezing. She had sneezed all night.

"Has Kathy taught you to tidy up already?" she asked Anna as she sorted through the clothes. "If so, it's a miracle! The number . . . oh dear! . . . the number . . . of times I've asked you to pick up . . . oh dear! oh dear! . . . your clothes! . . . Oh, this is awful! I seem to be sneezier than ever this morning . . . Oh!"

With that Anna's mother began sneezing in earnest. She sneezed until she had to sit down. She sneezed until she could not see. She sneezed until Anna was frightened and ran to the door to go for help. The first person she bumped into was Kathy, coming to see how Cotton Tail had got on through the night.

"Kathy! Kathy!" wailed Anna.

"What? What's the matter? What's happened to him?"

"It's not him! It's Mum! I don't know what to do!"

"Oh, I thought it was Cotton Tail!" said Kathy, sighing with relief. "What's the matter with your mum? She's not found him, has she?"

"She's sneezing and sneezing!"

"Is that all?"

"Terrible sneezing! Do people die of sneezing?"

"No," said Kathy firmly, wondering if Anna had gone mad.

"Come and see her," said Anna and dragged Kathy back to the flat.

They were just in time to hear her mother gasp, between explosions of sneezes, "It couldn't have been those books! Oh dear! Oh dear! If I didn't know better I would think there was a cat or rabbit or something in the house!"

"WHAT?" said Kathy and Anna together.

"Think there was a ... cat ... or a rabbit! Oh dear! Oh, excuse me, Kathy ... They're the only things I know ... Oh, this is terrible ... I'm allergic to ... Oh dear ..."

So that was the end of Cotton Tail's stay in Anna's bedroom. He was caught and handed over to Danny. Danny was quite happy to stay stroking him in the cupboard under the stairs while Anna and Kathy returned to Anna's bedroom and gave it a thorough de-rabbiting. This took all morning and while it was going on Anna's mother fell asleep on the sofa, overcome with exhaustion and the shock of Anna tidying up of her own free will for the first time in her life.

"Good heavens!" she said in amazement when they woke her up at lunchtime.

Anna's window had been opened wide and her bedroom was unrecognisable. It had been tidied and dusted and vacuumed and two bin bags full of rubbish had been removed from the floor.

"How do you feel?" asked Anna anxiously.

"Much better! Much, *much* better! Perhaps it *was* those books! Whatever made you decide to clear up your room at last?"

"We wondered if it was something in there that was making you sneeze," said Anna innocently.

"It was *very* dusty," said Kathy.

Anna's mother looked at them suspiciously for a moment, but was distracted by a knock on the door before she could say any more. It was Nathan with a message from Danny.

"He says, 'Are you coming down soon, and

what are you going to do now?' " he told Anna and Kathy.

"Oh," said Anna and Kathy, rather blankly.

"What *are* you going to do now?"

It was a question they had been asking each other all morning.

"We don't know," said Anna at last, and so slowly that her mother looked at her again.

"Something fishy is going on!" she said.

"Not fishy!" said Anna. "Not fishy at all . . ."

Chapter Four

They had another meeting in the cupboard under the stairs.

"Let's work it out," said Nathan. "Danny can't have him ..."

"I *can* have him later," interrupted Danny, who was looking forward very much to having Cotton Tail in his attic.

"Yes, but you can't have him *now*," said Nathan. "It's your fault! You've smuggled in too many animals and it's given your mum extra-sensory pet-detecting powers! And Kathy can't have him, they're decorating her room. You can't, Anna, your mum will sneeze her head off and anyway she's guessed something is up! Besides, your bedroom's no good now you've tidied it up. So it's either turn him in . . ."

"No! No!" said Kathy.

". . . or let me try having him!"

"But what about Chloe?"

"You girls will have to look after Chloe," said Nathan at once. "I've thought of that! I worked it all out this morning. Danny and I can pretend we're doing something private in my bedroom and we'll take care of the rabbit while you two keep Chloe out of the way! My mum will be really pleased! She's always wishing you would bother with Chloe more!"

"Is she really?"

"Oh yes," said Nathan. "You'll see!"

Nathan's mother was taken in by this plot but Chloe was not. She went straight to Kathy's jacket, lying across a chair, and inspected it very carefully, turning out the pockets and peering down the sleeves. Then she looked at her brother's closed bedroom door.

"Mine!" she announced, running over and pounding on it. "Mine, mine, mine, mine, mine!"

"Funny little thing!" said Nathan's mother, escaping to the kitchen. "I'll leave you girls to play!"

Cleaning Anna's bedroom had been hard, but it was nothing compared to the job of looking after Chloe that afternoon. Kathy and Anna played with dolls and bricks and jigsaws. They played ring-of-roses until it hurt to fall down. They played tea parties and hide-the-teddy and puppet shows. They read endless picture books. The moment a game stopped for even a second Chloe would run and hammer on Nathan's bedroom door shouting, "Mine! Mine! Mine!"

"I wonder what the boys have got in there that Chloe finds so exciting," remarked Nathan's mother, when she came in for a moment with drinks and biscuits. *Don't* do that, Chloe!"

Chloe ignored her and continued trying to stuff a large yellow fluffy duck under her jumper.

"She'll stretch her lovely new top!" said her mother. "Take it out please, Anna!"

Anna pulled it out and Chloe stuffed up a blue teddy instead. Then a pink rabbit. Then a black and white panda. Anna and Kathy took them all away and put them to bed behind the sofa where Chloe could not get to them and she lost her temper and returned to battering on Nathan's bedroom door.

"Leave us alone!" shouted Nathan through the keyhole.

"Mine, mine, mine!" shouted Chloe back.

"Can't you keep her quieter than that?"

"No we can't!" said Anna. "It's no good! We are both worn out and we can't keep it up any longer!"

"She'll go to bed in an hour or two!" called Nathan heartlessly.

"Yes, but what about tomorrow, and the next day and the next day? We can't keep this up for the rest of the week! And she's started stuffing animals up her jumper! What if someone guesses she's copying something she's seen? She's too clever, your sister!"

"She's not that clever!" said Nathan, opening the door a crack to peer out. "She's only one and a bit! Fancy being beaten by a one-year-old! Oh no, Chloe!"

Chloe had spotted the opening and she shot through it before anyone had time to stop her. After that there was chaos. She plunged after Cotton Tail, squealing with delight, and Cotton Tail ran in mad circles round and round the room until Kathy managed to catch him.

"Mine, mine, mine!" shrieked Chloe at the top of her voice.

"Guard the door, someone," ordered Anna, "before Nathan's mum comes to see what all the noise is about! Let Chloe stroke him, Kathy! Perhaps she'll shut up when she's had a proper look."

The trouble was that Chloe did not want to stroke Cotton Tail. She wanted to stuff him

up her jumper. Cotton Tail, however, was determined that this should not happen. He leapt from Kathy's arms and bolted under the bed.

"Mine, mine, mine!" wailed Chloe, throwing herself down on the floor.

"Shut *up*, Chloe!" begged Anna, trying to cuddle her into silence.

"Mine, mine, mine!" bawled Chloe.

"Whatever is going on in there?" demanded Mrs Amadi, rattling suddenly at the door handle. "Let me in!"

"Sorry, Mrs Amadi, we can't," called back Danny, leaning heavily on the door.

"Why ever not?"

"The door won't open!" shouted Nathan, from under his bed where he was trying to scoop out Cotton Tail.

"*Why* won't the door open?" demanded Mrs Amadi.

"There's something leaning on it," explained Danny, leaning harder than ever.

"Where's Chloe? Is she all right?"

"She's under the bed with Nathan," said Danny. "She's quite all right, Mrs Amadi, she . . ."

"Got you!" Mrs Amadi heard Nathan exclaim, and Chloe, who had been silent during the chase, began roaring again.

"Mine, mine, mine, MINE, MINE!"

"Whatever is *happening* to her?" shouted Mrs Amadi, losing patience. "Open this door at . . ."

The door did open just then, and Kathy, jacket on and head down, charged past her

at a run, tugged open the front door, and fled across the hall.

"Kathy!" exclaimed Mrs Amadi.

"She had to suddenly go," Nathan told her, trying to sound casual while he and Anna, clinging to an arm each, prevented Chloe from hurling herself after Kathy. "All at once! Like you saw!"

"Have you been fighting?" demanded his mother.

"No, no, no!"

"You've been up to something! Yes you have! I know that innocent look! That poor little girl! Give me Chloe at once. And go and make friends again before bedtime!"

Nathan, Anna and Danny were only too pleased to hand over Chloe, and they disappeared after Kathy at once. Mrs Amadi shook her head in bewilderment as she watched them go.

"They're back in that cupboard again," she told Chloe, hugging her. "They've got some secret . . ."

"Mine!" hiccuped Chloe pathetically. And Old McDonald came into the entrance hall just then and asked indignantly, "What's been happening to my friend Chloe? Who's been making her cry?"

"I'm afraid she seems to want something she can't have," explained Mrs Amadi.

"I hope you haven't got rid of that rocking horse!" said Old McDonald, suspicious at once. "That was a gift, that was, and one gratefully received, which is not what I usually get round here!"

"Mine!" remarked Chloe, sticking out her bottom lip and glaring at her mother.

"That's right, you stick up for yourself!" said Old McDonald.

"It wasn't the rocking horse," said Mrs Amadi hastily, "although I must talk to you about that because it fills up all the living room and I seem to walk into it every time I turn round . . ."

"Ho yes!" interrupted Old McDonald rudely. "I might have known!"

"Oh, please don't think I'm not grateful!"

"I bet you've not tried those saucepans either!"

"Well, I . . ."

"Nor got them rolls of carpet down!"

"But we *have* carpet already!"

"This is the thanks you get," said Old McDonald to Chloe. "None! That's what!"

In the cupboard under the stairs Danny said, "I'll have to have him! There's only me left!"

"But you said your mother would find him out straight away!" protested Kathy. "She's got extra-sensory pet-detecting powers, you said!"

"What else can we do?" asked Danny.

There did not seem to be anything else they could do and so Danny's mother was lured out of her flat, and while she was out of the way Cotton Tail was whisked up to the attic.

"It's the best place so far," admitted Kathy, looking around at the bare floor and the roof

tiles above. "I can make him a bed in a corner and put out his newspapers without having to hide them all the time. And he'll be able to have a good hop. He hasn't had a good hop for ages! It's nice!"

They were interrupted just then by the sound of Danny's mother's voice in the entrance hall below.

"Danny, where are you?" she called. "Nathan's just told me a load of rubbish about you needing me out in the garden . . ."

"Quick!" said Danny, and shoved Kathy down the attic stairs and followed as soon as he had shut the door behind him.

". . . I've been looking all over, thinking you'd hurt yourself, and now Anna tells me it was all a mistake . . ."

"Into the living room!" hissed Danny. "Kick off your shoes! Let me past and I'll switch on the telly as if we've been here for ages."

". . . and when I asked Nathan what it was all about he just stood there looking silly! Oh, hello Kathy! I didn't know you were here!

Take your feet *off* the sofa, Danny! Now, what *is* this all about?"

"What is *what* all about?" asked Danny.

"All this backwards and forwardsing . . ."

"Backwards and forwardsing?"

"And getting me out the way!"

"Getting you out the way?"

"As if I can't tell when you are up to something!"

"Up to something?"

"Don't just sit there, repeating everything I say!"

"I'm not! I'm not repeating everything you say!"

"Danny!"

"Can Nathan and Anna come up to play?"

"Play what?" asked his mother, rather taken aback to have the subject changed so suddenly.

"Hide and seek!"

"Charging about all over the flat? Oh no, thank you very much!"

"Darts?"

"Not until you've found a new place for that dart board! I remember it last time! Bang, bang, bang and holes all over the door!"

"Snap?"

"Has it *got* to be noisy games? Oh, all right! I suppose I can stand Snap!"

"You go and fetch them, Kathy!" ordered Danny. "Shout for them! Shout really loud!"

Kathy went at once. She knew what Danny had heard; she had heard it too. No wonder he suddenly needed to play noisy games. Cotton Tail was having a good hop at last.

"He must be exploring!" Kathy said urgently to Nathan and Anna. "He's bumping about up there and you can hear it plain as plain right through the ceiling! She'll notice any minute! It's only because Danny hasn't stopped talking that she hasn't found out already! He says to tell you to come up and play noisy games!"

The noisy games went on until nearly bedtime, with people being allowed home in relays to eat their suppers. It was a great relief when Danny's mother stuck her head round the bedroom door and announced that she could stand it no longer and was going down to Nathan's for a bit of peace.

"Thank goodness!" said Anna, dropping her snap cards on to the floor and collapsing on to Danny's bed. "This is the most tiring day of my life! Cleaning all morning and Chloe all afternoon and having to shout and crash about all night!"

"Shut up and listen for a minute!" ordered Nathan.

"Why?"

"It's gone quiet," said Danny. "Cotton Tail's asleep at last!"

Kathy would not leave without checking that this was true, and so very, very silently they left Danny's bedroom, unlocked the door of the attic stairs, climbed stealthily up and lifted the trapdoor.

"There!" whispered Anna, pointing, and they all gazed at the corner where Cotton Tail lay stretched out on Kathy's old jacket, fast asleep. Then they all crept down again and closed the attic door.

"Bed time at last!" said Anna, sighing with relief.

Chapter Five

In the middle of the night Danny's mother woke up. She could hear bumping. It was coming from somewhere overhead. The bumping started and stopped, and started and stopped again. There was a rustling papery sound, and then silence. Then more bumps. Then scratching, like claws.

Danny's mother thought of her son's animal madness. She remembered his strange behaviour that afternoon. Also she remembered the time he had started a zoo in the attic and the time, shortly afterwards, when the roof had blown off.

"Not again!" moaned Danny's mother.

The bumping came and went, near and

then far away, and then very far away, so that she could not be quite sure whether she had really heard it or not. Danny's mother began to get sleepy.

"I must have been dreaming!" she told herself. "Having a nightmare! He wouldn't dare!"

At that moment the scratching came again, very loudly, and right over her head. Danny's mother stopped being sleepy and thought all at once, and very clearly, of rats. Rats, along with spiders, were her least favourite animals in the world. Not that that would stop Danny bringing them home, thought his mother, and she jumped out of bed and ran into Danny's room and shouted, "DANIEL O'BRIEN, WHAT HAVE YOU PUT IN THAT ATTIC?"

"I dunno," groaned Danny sleepily. "Go 'way!"

"There are noises! Terrible noises!"

"Are there?" asked Danny, waking up a bit more.

"Rats! Is it rats?"

"'Course not," said Danny, rubbing his eyes and wondering what on earth to do.

"You've put something up there!"

"I haven't," said Danny, remembering thankfully that it was Kathy, not himself, who had carried Cotton Tail upstairs.

"Just listen!"

Danny listened and heard no sound at all. No bumping, no rustling and no scratching.

"Can't hear a thing!" he said solemnly.

"It stops and starts," said his mother. "There's some animal up there, I know there is! I'm going to look!"

"There's spiders!" said Danny, suddenly inspired. "I don't know if you could hear them though, but there are loads of spiders! I went up not long ago and I noticed then that there was an *awful* lot of . . ."

"I thought I told you not to go into that attic!"

"Well, I know, but I did. I just went to look. I wondered if there were any spiders left now we've got a new roof. I thought they might have all gone. But there's thousands . . ."

Danny watched his mother hopefully. She was terrified of spiders.

"Perhaps there were spiders' *eggs* left behind when the roof blew off. Perhaps that's where they've all come from. Perhaps they hatched . . ."

"Uh! Shut up, Danny!"

"I didn't see any rats though!" Danny yawned. "Are you really going to look?"

"I ought to," said his mother, but she sounded far less determined than she had a few minutes earlier.

"What would you do if there was a rat?" asked Danny cunningly.

"Die of fright."

"I don't think you ought to go then," said Danny, snuggling down into his pillow.

"Perhaps I could ask Old McDonald to have a look in the morning," said his mother. "Perhaps that would be better! Only I know what he'll be like if I do! Horrible! Asking

about the sofa and whether I've got that dreadful fly curtain up yet . . . I'm sorry, Danny! You're tired! Go to sleep!"

"Mmmmm" said Danny, and he managed to sound so sleepy that his mother forgot that only a few minutes earlier she had suspected him of bringing home rats.

"Sweet dreams!" she whispered, and bent down and tucked him up as carefully as if he had been two years old again.

Danny did not go to sleep. He lay awake for what felt like hours and hours, devising a plan of such cunning that in the morning he could hardly believe it was his own invention.

Anna, Nathan and Kathy (with Cotton Tail once again stuffed inside her jacket) listened in disbelief.

"Bonkers," they said. "Completely crazy. Crackers. Nuts. Barmy. Danny's gone mad. Poor old Danny. Totally lost it this time."

"I don't know though," said Nathan slowly. "When you think about it, it might just work."

"You too?" asked Anna and Kathy. "Boys! Typical. Chloe's got more sense than that."

"Actually," said Anna, "it's not a bad idea. Especially if the grown ups *will* help."

"Would they?" asked Kathy.

"Let's ask them," said Anna.

Danny's mother was the first to be asked. She listened to the whole story, from the knocking over of Chloe to the night-time noises in the attic, and she exclaimed,

"DANNY O'BRIEN, ARE YOU SITTING THERE TELLING ME YOU KNEW IT WAS A RABBIT ALL THE TIME?"

"Well, yes," said Danny.

"Where is it now?"

Danny pointed to Kathy and she obligingly unzipped her jacket so that Danny's mother could see.

"Good grief!" said Danny's mother.

"He's called Cotton Tail," Kathy told her.

"How long has he been in Paradise House?"

"Three nights," said Kathy. "One in my room, one in Anna's and last night . . ."

"In the attic," finished Danny's mother. "Frightening me to death!"

"Sorry," said Kathy.

"I thought it was rats!" said Danny's mother, and then, seeing Kathy's indignant face, added kindly, "But he's a lovely rabbit! I've never seen such a nice one! What are you going to do with him now?"

"We've got a lovely plan to keep him," said

Danny. "But it will work much better if the grown ups help."

"Oh no! Oh no, oh no!" said Danny's mother at once. "No secret rabbits for me!"

"What we want you to do," said Nathan, ignoring this protest, "is say 'Thank you' to Old McDonald."

"And hang up the beady curtain," said Anna. "After all, it will be useful for keeping out flies!"

"You *sound* like Old McDonald!"

"And let me keep the sofa," said Danny. "It's a very comfy sofa! Much too good to throw away!"

"But why?" asked Danny's mother.

"Old McDonald says you should say 'Thank you' when you are given a present," explained Danny. "Even if you don't really want it. He says it's manners!"

"I haven't noticed that Old McDonald's manners are all that sparkling," remarked his mother.

"If people are nice about *his* presents,"

explained Danny patiently, "then perhaps he will be nice when he gets presents back."

"Are you planning to give Old McDonald a present?" asked Danny's mother.

"Yes," said everyone, and she suddenly understood and began to laugh.

"Of course I'll say 'Thank You'," she agreed.

Kathy had to stay outside while they explained to Anna's mother.

"So it *was* a rabbit!" she said. "I might have known! Anna, you terrible child!"

"I didn't know you were allergic to rabbits – not until you said," said Anna, embarrassed.

"And I blamed Old McDonald's books and gave them all back! And he was so cross! I don't suppose he'll ever forgive me!"

"He will if you ask for them back."

"It would be a big help if you asked for them back," agreed Danny earnestly. "Because Old McDonald thinks that when people are given things, even if they are

things they don't really want, they should be pleased. Not moan and say they're a nuisance. It would be a shame if someone, say one of us, gave Old McDonald a present and he just moaned and said it was a nuisance!"

"What are you thinking of giving Old McDonald?" asked Anna's mother. "And what has all this got to do with Kathy's rabbit?"

"Everything," said Nathan and Danny and Anna.

Nathan's mother was in the entrance hall, touching up the rocking horse with red and gold and silver paint.

"Mine!" said Chloe approvingly, as she watched.

"I'm going to stand it out here on those rugs you gave me!" Nathan's mother told Old McDonald. "And I should have thanked you properly for those saucepans! Proper copper bottoms! I polished them all up this morning!

Hullo, Nathan! What did you want?"

"Nothing," said Nathan. "I was going to ask you to do something, but you've done it already."

"Old McDonald," said Nathan later on that morning, "can we give you something?"

Nathan had been chosen to speak, because of all the Paradise House children, he had been the first to make friends with Old McDonald. Kathy stood beside him because it was her rabbit. Anna was in front – she had been given the job of knocking on the basement door – and Danny was hovering nervously behind, hoping and hoping that his plan would work.

"Ho," said Old McDonald. "One, two, three, four of you now! Made friends then, have you?"

"We made friends ages ago!" said Anna.

"I should think so too! And how is your mum getting on with them books?"

"She's left them for Dad to unpack.

He's sitting on the floor reading them. Mum's upstairs helping Danny's mum hang up that beady curtain. And now we've brought something that we want to give to you."

"You might not want it," said Nathan.

"You might not know what to do with it," said Danny.

"You might say 'No'," said Kathy. "And then I don't know what I'd do. It's a rabbit. It's my rabbit."

"Ho!" said Old McDonald.

"You're allowed to keep pets, aren't you?" said Danny pleadingly. "Not like us. You said it's different for you because you're the caretaker."

"He's got a hutch. Kathy's dad says he'll drive down and fetch it straight away if you say 'Yes'."

"We'll clean him out. And feed him and look after him and everything."

"Ho!" said Old McDonald again.

"Chloe loves him!"

"Wouldn't you like a rabbit for a present?" asked Kathy.

"This is a set-up!" said Old McDonald. "Four on to one! Four on to one is disgraceful!"

"He's joking!" whispered Nathan to Kathy.

"Lucky for you I have always wanted a rabbit!"

"Have you? Have you really?"

"From a boy," said Old McDonald solemnly. "On and off! You tell your dad to go and collect that hutch!"

"Oh, thank you!" exclaimed Kathy and Danny and Nathan and Anna. "Thank you! Thank you!"

"Thank *you*!" said Old McDonald, very politely.